Merry Christmas, Teletubbies!

From the original TV scripts
by Andrew Davenport.

SCHOLASTIC INC.

New York Toronto London Auckland Sydney Mexico City New Delhi Hong Kong

ISBN 0-439-10596-X

12 11 10 9 8 7 6 5 4 3 2 1   9/9 0/0 1/0 2/0 3/0

Illustrated by Tim Jacobus
Designed by Joan Ferrigno

Printed in Mexico

First Scholastic printing, November 1999

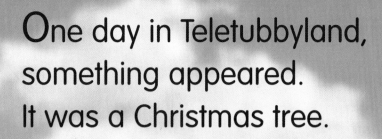

One day in Teletubbyland,
something appeared.
It was a Christmas tree.

Four presents appeared on the tree.
One for Tinky Winky. One for Dipsy.
One for Laa-Laa. And one for Po.

Po decided to open her present.

Oooh! Po open present!

jingle
jangle

It was a little frosty cloud.

The little frosty
cloud began to snow.
Tinky Winky, Dipsy, Laa-Laa, and Po
loved the snow.

The Teletubbies went inside.
Laa-Laa wanted to open her present.

Oooh! Laa-Laa open present!

jingle jangle

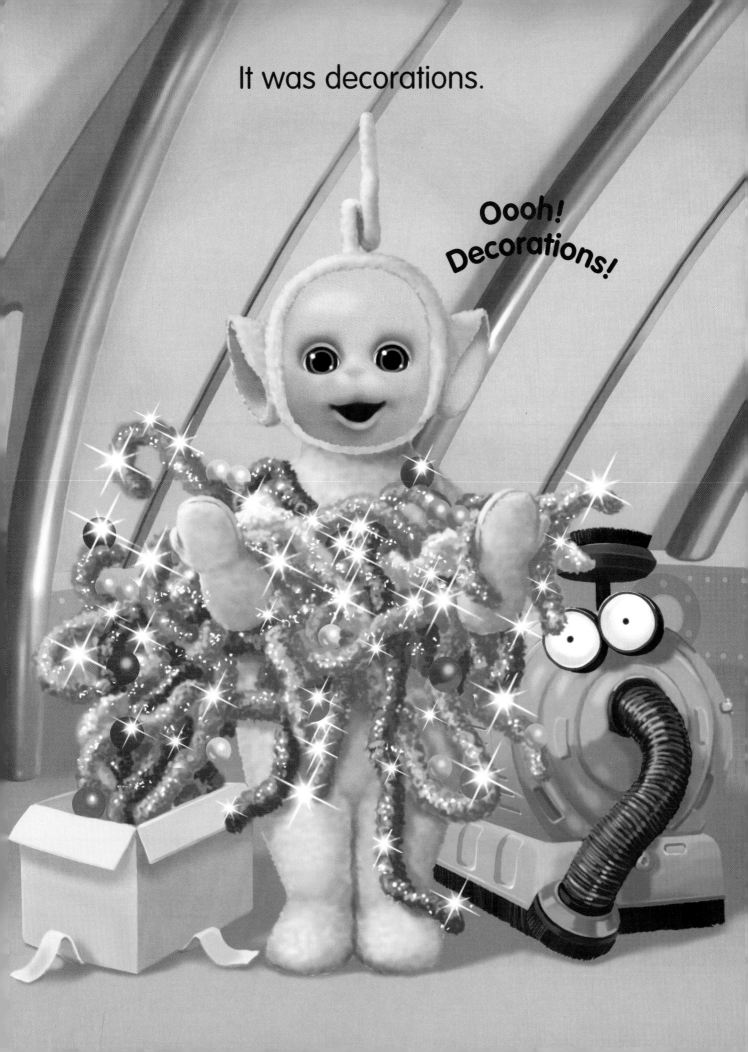

But the Noo-noo decided to tidy up.

The decorations made the Tubbytronic Superdome very festive.

How festive!

Then Dipsy decided to open his present.

Oooh! Dipsy open present!

jingle
jangle

Tinky Winky, Laa-Laa, and Po
all helped Dipsy open the cracker.

Then Tinky Winky decided
to open his present.

Oooh! Tinky Winky
open present!

jingle
jangle

Tinky Winky, Dipsy, Laa-Laa, and Po
followed the star . . .

Star!

. . . all the way to the Christmas tree.

Merry Christmas, Teletubbies!

Merry Christmas!